The Librarian Checked Out

by

K.J.Goss

SHIRES PRESS

4869 Main Street
P.O. Box 2200
Manchester Center, VT 05255
www.northshire.com

The Librarian Checked Out

ISBN Number: 978-0-9997533-3-0

Building Community, One Book at a Time
*A family-owned, independent bookstore in
Manchester Ctr., VT, since 1976 and Saratoga Springs, NY since 2013.
We are committed to excellence in bookselling.
The Northshire Bookstore's mission is to serve as a resource for
information, ideas, and entertainment while honoring the needs of
customers, staff, and community.*

Printed in the United States of America

The Librarian Checked Out

Day one.

A brisk fall day, though with a comfortable temperature welcomed the city's working population on this Monday morning. Harold Twining walked up the many steps of the public library. He knew he was a few minutes late which did not bother him knowing the Director, Florence Goodwyn, was always early to open up. Harold was the assistant director and had been for several years. He knew his job well and performed his duties with the utmost precision.

As he reached the top step he saw Joyce Lambertson, the head librarian of Science studies waiting by the locked door.

"Good morning Joyce. What are you doing out here ? I figured you would be well into your routine by now."

Smiling her answer;

"I remembered halfway here that I left my key in my desk on Friday. No matter I thought, Florence is always here early. Obviously she's late also. It must have been a hectic weekend for all of us."

Chuckling at her remarks Harold fumbled with his keys. Finding the correct one he unlocked the door and stepped aside to allow Joyce first entry.

"Thank you kind sir." she smiled

The two each went their own way once inside to start the usual routine, Harold to the small kitchenette to start the coffee and Joyce to the main light switch panel and methodically flipped all the breakers on. Being a Monday it would be rare for any patrons to come in this early so she headed for the locker room to hang up her sweater. A last minute check in the mirror assured her that her hair was all neat and in place. She exited the locker room as Harold was coming in.

"No sign of Flo yet?" she asked for the sake of conversation only.

"Not yet." Harold mumbled.

Joyce went right to the front reception desk awaiting Harold's return before she continued her opening preparations. Checking the clock she realized it would still be another ten minutes before the other help arrived. While waiting she checked the drop box and retrieved three books which she brought to the central desk. Bringing the computer on line she signed in for the day. At two minutes to the hour the four remaining employees walked through the door. After the usual good morning rituals Joyce excused herself, proceeding to her assigned department.

The Department of Science Studies occupied a large area on the second floor. She pushed back the large pocket door exposing the area of tables and chairs for the convenience of researchers. The walls were, of course, lined with shelves from floor to ceiling all filled with subjects of the various sciences. The right side wall also contained a single wide pocket door secreting the more important and rare books of the ancients. These were neatly held by rolling stacks, or compact shelving to be more correct, in an environment of temperature and humidity control. The stacks, naturally, were locked together for additional security. Lilly, one of the young assistants recovered the key from its safe place and unlocked the stacks. Struggling a few times to slide the shelving apart it appeared to be jammed somehow.

"Joyce." she called softly, "I can't seem to open the stacks."

Joyce, a bit annoyed at being disturbed stood from her desk and walked to the room indicating that Lily should step aside. Pushing her normal way on the handle moved nothing. She looked at Lily with the message she should help. Each gripping a separate stack they pulled away from each other. A third effort, with much strain, finally proved successful. The shelves were now free rolling.

A quick intake of breath before there were mutual screams which broke the silence of the library. Lily turned and ran heading for where she did not know. Joyce remained glued to her spot, visibly shaking, as she stared at the crushed body of Florence Goodwyn, the face grotesquely twisted in serious pain. By the time she was able to move Harold was at her side. Enfolding Joyce in his arms he gently turned her head away from a view no one should have to witness.

One of the other assistants arrived and relieved Harold of his shocked burden. Instantly he went to the phone dialing 911. Returning downstairs he instructed the others to put up a sign that the library was closed due to an emergency and to lock the doors. All gathered in the main lobby area awaiting the police. Joyce had calmed somewhat with the care of two of the young girls but was still visibly shaking with tears flowing.

$\sim \sim \sim \sim$

In just under ten minutes the police were there, three uniformed officers and two plain cloths men entered. One of the uniformed men stationed himself outside the door.

Harold took over introducing himself. Leaving the others in the company of a uniform he led the remainder upstairs. What they saw took even them, experienced as they were, by surprise. Here was a fairly attractive woman in her mid fifties, her neck wired tightly to an upper shelf, her arms outstretched and wired to another shelf while her feet were wired to the bottom. Indentations and bruising showed through out the whole body without the presence of quantities of blood.

Mark Dwyer, the plainclothes Detective Sergeant, after a quick examination directed his assistant to call the medical examiner. His further instructions were not to disturb the body until the ME completed his preliminary exam. Another uniform was posted by the stack room door. Sgt. Dwyer and his partner returned to the first floor to interview the employees.

"I know this is difficult for you all but it is necessary for us to gather whatever information we can. We are going to take individual statements so please be patient. We will have you all on your way as soon as possible. Mr. Twining if you will join me, Sgt. Conrad will talk to Joyce, I believe you said ?"

Joyce nodded in the affirmative. She then followed Sgt.

Conrad to a quiet corner away from the others. Joyce was surprised by the sensitivity and concern that Hank Conrad showed. He was gentle with the questions and appeared satisfied with her answers.

Over in another corner was Sgt. Dwyer with Harold Twining. Dwyer's questions were more direct and with an official air about them.

"Yes Sgt. The last time I saw Florence, I mean Ms. Goodwyn was Friday about noon. I left early because I had a flight to Philadelphia for a business meeting."

"What sort of business if I might ask ?" said the Sgt.

"Not a problem." replied Harold willingly. "I was to meet someone regarding an old first edition possibly for sale. I stayed in Philly both Friday and Saturday nights arriving back here late Sunday."

Can this be corroborated by witnesses ?" was the follow up question.

"Most certainly, I don't have the tickets with me but I can get them from home."

"I don't mean just airline tickets. I'm speaking of physical witnesses."

"Most certainly, I can give you the name and address of the gentleman I was meeting with if you wish."

"Not right now." replied the Sgt. "But give it to one of the uniformed officers before you leave. How long have you worked here and how well did you know the deceased ?"

"I've been here about six years, the last three as assistant director. I was acquainted with Florence for a few years through mutual societies and organizations to which we both belonged. I only learned to really know her after I came to work here. Our relationship, though very friendly, never went beyond this work place. Our social lives were strictly our own."

"Can you think of any reason why anyone would want to kill her, especially in this fashion ?"

"Most certainly not Sgt.." answered Harold in a positive and affirmative tone. You ask that as if you were accusing me of such a dastardly deed"

"I am by no means implying that, I assure you sir." replied Dwyer quickly.

Harold not really listening to the Sgt continued, "She was

admired and well liked by both the staff and the public she interacted with and served well. This is most distressing. I feel for poor Joyce over there. She looked up to Florence almost like a mother."

"I guess that will be all for now." finished Sgt. Dwyer. "Except for the usual warning of don't leave town."

"I don't plan on going anywhere Sgt. After all we still have a library to run. You would be surprised at how much the public requires and relies on our services and naturally the board of directors will have to be notified. I guess I had better get to that right away."

Mark Dwyer stood and walked away while Harold was still talking, thinking to himself that Harold was a self appointed wind bag.

Sgt. Conrad finished with Joyce about the same time. Harold then took over the comforting of Joyce while the other two girls were being interviewed.

The Medical Examiner arrived with his team along with a fingerprint group. Dwyer led them to the second floor crime scene. Dr. Johanson's first remark was, "This is a new one on me and I have certainly seen a lot in my years with the Department."

"Can you come up with a time of death ?" asked Sgt. Conrad.

"Naturally I'll know more later but just with my first observation I would say forty eight to seventy two hours ago. I'll pin it down exactly once we get back to the lab.

Dwyer and Conrad left the ME to do his job with instructions to the officer out side the room that there would be no one allowed in until further notice. The pair returned to the first floor. Mark Dwyer released the staff telling Twining the library was to remain closed until further notice. Instantly Harold objected rather vehemently coming up with a thousand reasons to keep it open. The Sgt. Did not budge from his decision, in fact insisted that meant Harold also.

Stomping off in a huff Twining was heard to mumble "We'll see about this. The board of directors and police commissioner will hear about this."

"I was right when I said windbag." Mark whispered to himself as he trekked upstairs to join the ME.

~ ~ ~ ~

Well, Johanson what do you think."

"It is unique, I'll give you that. replied Johanson.

The body had been taken down and wrapped in a black body bag.

"This is going to be an interesting autopsy." continued Johanson. "I'm pretty much finished here, I'll get out of your way and let your lab people do their thing."

"Thanks Doc. See you later."

As the doctor walked away Sgt. Susan Blake approached. "Hi Mark."

"Susan." he answered in recognition.

"Now that Doc. is out of the way we should be able to wrap this up in three or four hours. I had one of the guys get staff fingerprints before they left."

"Good thinking." commented Dwyer. "Get back to me as soon as possible, I just know the commissioner is going to be jumping on this one."

Susan smiled as she returned to her team.

Mark joined his own men downstairs. Hank Conrad met him at the stairway. "There's not much more we can do right now. We checked both the side and rear exits. Both were locked and barred from the inside. There is no sign of forced entry."

"Oh great." sighed Sgt. Dwyer. "Just what we need, a possible inside job that we will have no fingerprints for except for the staff. On top of that it's a public building."

"Glad to see you're so upbeat about it." smiled Conrad.

Both men were silent while they each were making notes in their on site reports.

"Something still doesn't fit right." said Dwyer out loud. "The front door was locked, the side and back doors are barred from the inside and only three people have keys." As if in a rush he added."Hank, have some of the men check all the windows and at the same time check every nook and cranny in this place."

"Looking for what ?" questioned Hank.

"I don't know." Mark mumbled. "Perhaps the killer who hasn't left yet ?"

Thirty minutes later Sgt. Conrad reentered the main lobby.

Dwyer looked up from his notes to see the expression on Hank's face that he did not want to see.

"No luck any where Mark, and we checked everything except between the book pages. And to add to the mystery we found the deceased purse. Her keys to the place are still there."

"Damn." shouted Mark. That sort of says it was one of the staff, but only two of them have keys. The blowhard has an alibi and I have my doubts about the woman Joyce. Those sobs and tears seemed genuine, although I'm not ruling anybody out.

Conrad interrupted. "Oh yeah, that reminds me. We checked with that woman Joyce. It seems she left her keys in her desk when she left on Friday. We checked that out and sure enough there they were.

"Oh great." was the frustrated sigh from Mark. "I knew I should have stayed in bed this morning." Just finishing the sentence Dwyers' cell phone rang. "Dwyer here." were the only two words spoken after that he just listened while his face grew red. Hank knew then this was not good news. "In about an hour." Mark finally answered and clicked off the phone.

Hank knew it was not possible but he thought he saw smoke coming out of his partners ears.

"That SOB. It certainly didn't take him long."

"Who ?" inquired Hank.

"The windbag of an Assistant Director. He must have run all the way to headquarters when he left here. I now have to report to the Captain as soon as I get back."

Leaving Sgts. Conred and Blake to finish up with firm instructions to have at least two men to look after the place twenty four hours a day, Mark exited the building.

"This fall air feels good. Let's hope it can refresh me long enough to face the Captain." he said aloud to himself.

~ ~ ~ ~ ~ ~

Captain Bradick was stern, but known to be fair. "Help yourself to coffee and sit down, we obviously have to talk." Braddick directed.

Dwyer did as he was told mentally working on staying calm.

"Okay, now fill me in as to what transpired between you and Harold Twining."

Mark Dwyer slowly relayed the whole story in as much detail as possible, not high lighting his encounter with the assistant Director.

"Sounds like good standard police proceedure to me." commented Braddick.

Mark felt somewhat relieved until the word "BUT" came from the Captains lips.

"Apparently this Mr. Twining has friends in high places. In this short period of time I have heard from the Mayor, the DA and the Commissioner. Now exactly what took place between you and Twining"

Finishing his coffee and taking a deep breath Mark could feel his anger rising. He took an extra minute to compose himself before speaking. As calmly as he could he reiterated almost word for word the conversation between he and Harold Twining.

"According to the Commissioner you accused him of the murder.." Braddick stated.

"I did no such thing, Captain. I know better than that. But I will tell you this, he is presently number one on the suspect list."

"He said he has an alibi."

"So he says, but which has yet to be checked out. Look Captain." Mark said softly. "We're only into this not even four hours yet. At least give us some time to work. The only thing we have for certain is a dead body. Preliminary statements from a few people does not an investigation make. If the commissioner is so hot to trot to defend Twining let him take over the whole investigation."

"This last remark Mark made in a slightly raised voice. Braddick raised his hand quickly.

"Okay Mark, calm down. You have convinced me and I'm on your side. Tell you what, continue with what you're doing and I'll take care of the upper echelon people. Just promise to keep me in the loop with every detail. I'll back you all the way. I know your reputation as a detective and I respect your moves and decisions."

Feeling a bit guilty for almost losing it he apologized to the Captain and thanked him.

Dwyer left Braddicks office and stopped at the coffee machine before heading to his own cubby of an office. This was shared with Hank Conrad. They had worked as a team for a few years and worked well together. With his notes in front of him he sipped his coffee and ran the morning through his mind. He realized this was doing no good. He had to wait for something more concrete both from the Medical Examiner and the lab tech's. He reached for some old paperwork to keep occupied until Hank returned.

It was close to five PM when Hank Conrad, somewhat bedraggled looking, entered the cubby hole office.

"I didn't expect you to be this late." Dwyer commented.

"Neither did I but Blake and her team really got into it. I asked what was the holdup. She laughed her answer, "We can't find any thing out of the ordinary.""

Mark sighed with disappointment again.

"She insisted on going over everything a second, third and forth time."

"And ?" queried Mark.

"She said she maybe had something but wouldn't say what until she did some lab testing. I guess we're just going to have to wait for tomorrow. How did you make out with the Captain ?"

"It could have been worse. It seems Twining went right to the Mayor, the DA and Commissioner. That of course triggered a ripple effect which ended with Braddick and then of course me or us. We're going to have to tread softly for a while."

"That may not be too easy."

Mark looked at Hank questioningly.

"I don't know how it happened but on the way back I heard our little incident on the news already."

"You're kidding I hope." stated Mark.

"It wasn't any of our people." said Hank.

"Wait here, let me inform Braddick of this before he jumps on us again."

Braddick turned off his small TV as Dwyer entered his office. The Captain spoke first.

"I know what you're going to say, I just saw it on the news."

"It wasn't us Captain."

"I didn't think it was and don't worry. I said I'll take care of the upper brass and I will. But I am going to schedule a press conference for tomorrow afternoon. That gives you time to put something together without divulging anything critical.

"Oh thanks." Mark replied.

"You can go now." smiled Braddick.

Back in his own office addressing Hank; "Let's hope we can come up with something by tomorrow afternoon. We're going to a press conference and I'm the spokesperson according to the Captain. And wipe that smile off your face." Mark said with a grin of his own.

"Oh, by the way, while waiting for Susan to finish we checked the exterior of the building including the roof."

"And." waited Mark.

"Nothing, absolutely nothing. Everything was as it should be."

"Any other wonderful news." Mark asked sarcastically.

"No but personally I think we should interview the staff again. In minute detail this time."

"I agree, see what you can do to set that up. Let's try and do it here in our interview rooms."

"Got it." Hank replied. "In the meantime I'm going home to a good supper and a beer. Care to join me. You know how good a cook my wife is."

"Thanks but no. I have a few more things to checkout first, then I'll probably get Chinese on the way home."

"Your loss." Hank replied over his shoulder leaving.

Day two.

It was six forty five Tuesday morning as Mark opened the door to his office. He barely put his coffee cup down when Sgt. Susan Blake appeared at his door.

"Oh good, you're in." she greeted.

"And good morning to you too, Susan." Mark answered. "You're in early."

"I didn't go home yet." she admitted. "Can you come down to the lab ? I want you to see something."

"Good news I hope." he said reaching for his coffee.

"I don't know. It's something that has kept me baffled all night."

She explained to Mark as they walked to the lab. "I was becoming frustrated because I couldn't find anything I could call interesting until we were ready to pack it in."

"Now you really have my interest. Go on."

"Wait a few minutes, I would rather show you."

The lab was void of people, the day shift had not come in yet. Susan had worked alone all night. "We did the usual finger print routine which netted us nothing. True there were a few non staff prints, which, of course we will check out, but they didn't set off any alarms because of how and where we found them. It was then I noticed a disturbance on the floor. It was dirt, But on closer inspection it was not ordinary dirt. I know some people would say dirt is dirt but there is a significant difference if you know what you're looking at. I had a forensics mentor years ago who drilled certain things into my head. He drove me crazy years ago but in retrospect I'm glad he hounded me." Correcting herself she continued, "Forgive me for getting carried away.

Mark politely smiled.

"Getting back to the present I don't know what drew me to it but from old teachings, never let anything go by no matter how insignificant. The sample I'm referring to was minute but something inside me said to look at it. As I was scraping a sample for the lab I noticed a few other almost undetectable spots between the rolling stacks and the stairway. I followed these minute spots to a back hallway where they just disappeared."

Mark was intrigued by her story so far.

"Now for the bast part. Once we came back here to the lab I started my analysis. As I mentioned before dirt is dirt unless it is blended or combined with another ingredient.

"Mark was starting to lose her. Susan detected this saying;

"Bear with me a little longer, please."

Again Dwyer just smiled and nodded. Sgt. Blake resumed without hesitation.

"Add water to a dirt mixture and you get mud. Throw in a third and possibly a fourth ingredient and you get a distinctive mixture that indicates its source. Now if you will Mark, look into the microscope. This is the unique spot I was talking evidence.."

Mark looked into the scope to see a moist gray black smear hosting many microbes. Pulling his head away he turned to Susan, questions in his eyes. She sat down answering slowly.

"Normal dirt or gravel from patrons shoes cab be found every where including here in our own headquarters. But what you just observed is from sewage."

Mark really was puzzled now.

"Could it have been from patrons shoes ?"

"Possibly but I think not. Even if you stepped in raw sewage, by the time you walked on regular roads and sidewalks it would all but disappear before you entered the library. There are no traces of it in the building except where I mentioned earlier. And even if it was found it would not show the consistency that you just viewed. It would be all but dried. I'm not just guessing at this Mark. I did the lab studies of a case from two years or so ago. I know what I'm looking at. No Mark this is fresh and limited to a certain section of the library not normally traveled by patrons. It may be nothing but I think it should be checked out."

"I have to agree with you on that. We have nothing else to go on yet, at least this is a start."

"Oh by the way, I took the liberty of cordoning off the areas in question so this evidence doesn't get contaminated.

"Great work Blake. Get this all written up and go home and get some sleep. We'll check with each other again tomorrow."

Susan smiled, proud of herself and agreed on going home.

While Sgt. Blake started on her report of her findings, Mark took another peek in the microscope before going back to his office. No sooner entering his cubby hole when Hank joined him. They each fixed their coffee and Dwyer reiterated Blake's findings to Conrad.

"Wow, that's some findings. Kudos to Susan. Okay based on that I'll take a few uniforms and give a thorough look see on the outside perimeter and I guess in the basement also."

"That would be a great help to me, I have to prepare for the stupid press conference."

"Did you hear who told the press of this."

"To be perfectly honest, no. When I finally did leave last night I had dinner and went to bed without radio or television." answered Mark matter of factly

"It was none other than your favorite Mr. Twinning. It was on the eleven o'clock news. He gave sort of a mini interview and boy was he eating up the notoriety. He was making himself out to be the savior of the Public Library. You know, how he was going to have the library open as quickly as possible to serve the needs of the citizens."

"Oh brother, just what we need, more interference. I'm going to make his alibi first on my list today. Okay Hank, you go do what you want at the crime scene, I'm going to talk to the Captain. And remember, no one, and I mean no one enters the building. Double check what Susan said she roped off, that area is strictly forbidden except to you, me and Blake."

"Gotcha" Mark heard Hank say as he left the office.

~ ~ ~ ~ ~ ~

"I'm sure you know by now Sir who it was that went to the press." said Sgt. Dwyer.

"Yes, and I have already been in touch with the

Commissioner. He is going to speak with the DA and the Mayor. Hopefully we can shut him up a little with out getting into trouble for trying to squelch the freedom of the press."

"That would be a great help Captain and thank you. Now as far as the press conference I'm going to use the standard white wash stuff, that is with your permission of course. I can't really say much anyway because we don't have anything to go on yet. It is much to early, we have barely started our investigation. By the way Blake may have found something but at this point even that is ninety five percent questionable. We just need time."

"You will have all the time you need, but remember to keep me informed."

Sgt. Dwyer left the Captains office feeling more secure with Braddicks obvious support. He had a few hours before the One o'clock press gathering. This gave him the time necessary to find out who the Board of Directors were for the library and gather contact information. This lead he would definitely follow personally. After recording all the information regarding the directors he checked the time. Not enough to start seeking them and so changed priorities and went to see the ME. Doctor Johanson had recently completed some blood analysis and was at the computer at his desk.

"Oh Mark, I was about to call you. I have some new information that you might find interesting.

"Right now I'll take anything I can get." replied Dwyer.

"Obviously, as we both know, the cause of actual death was being crushed in the sliding stacks. I started thinking to myself how would one go about wiring a body to those shelves with out resistance or a sign of struggle. The woman didn't weigh much , a mere one hundred twelve pounds., but it would be dead weight. That would be a struggle even for a strong man."

"I understand that much but what point are you trying to make." asked Mark quietly.

"That is the point." Johanson answered. "How would you go about such a thing without help."

"Are you saying there was more than one person ?"

"Not necessarily. Which is why I did some blood samples."

"And." Mark anxiously awaited.

"She was drugged into cooperation."

"What." the Sergeant said rather loud. "Who would or could

cooperate knowing it meant their death.”

“The drug used is not new but it is not well known either. It has been used in mental wards for some of the more severe patients. It seriously calms them down and makes them more cooperative.”

“You mean more like zombies.” Dwyer commented sarcastically.

“That’s a rather harsh description but I guess you could compare it to that. Being in the medical field I wouldn’t quite put it that way. Behavior modification is sometimes necessary.” Calmly answered Johanson.

“Sorry Doc. I didn’t mean to get that crude. You sort of took me by surprise. So if I understand correctly, the killer administered this drug so the victim would willingly do certain things.”

“In a nutshell, that is essentially correct. That would then enable a lone person to accomplish what we witnessed.”

“I almost find that difficult to believe, but then again so far everything about this is weird, so why not accept that also.”

Johanson smiled at Mark understanding his frustration.

The actual or official cause of death was asphyxiation for obvious reasons but this was a long time planed thing. Premeditated without a doubt.”

“Okay, that tells us we must now go over her place of residence with a fine tooth comb. Hopefully we can find something to give us a lead to who. Thanks Doc. I’ll leave you to finish up whatever you do. Please let me know if you came across or think of anything else that might help.”

The doctor nodded his agreement as Mark stood to leave.

~ ~ ~ ~ ~ ~

Entering the press room Mark received relatively chilled looks from his favorite trio, the Mayor, the DA and the Commissioner. Braddick instantly grabbed his arm ushering him to the podium. His only words were,

“Don’t worry about them. Just feed the press something to keep them away for a while.”

Ten minutes later Dwyer was leaving via the back door to avoid further questions from the press. He met both Conrad and Braddick at his office.

"Good job with the press and I already spoke to Johanson. I'll let you two get busy, I know you have a difficult problem with this one."

The Captain turned and left without a further word leaving Hank and Mark staring at each other. It was now two forty five as both Sgts. threw themselves into their respective chairs.

"You first." Mark said.

"Okay - I have absolutely nothing to report. The place is clean of anything for us to even think about. The only thing there was what Blake discovered.

"Kind of what I expected but I was hoping for more." Dwyer then mentioned the Board of Directors and what he learned from the ME.

Hank was as surprised as Mark at Doc's findings.

"So either the Doc is right or we can look for two people, possibly three." he replied.

"I thought of that possibility also. It's only been two days and already I wish I was a beat cop again."

Hank chuckled as he spoke.

"But you're not and you love what you're doing."

Mark also chuckled. "Do you think we can start the detailed interviews today ?"

Hank answered affirmatively. "I'm going to leave Twining to you and schedule him last."

"Good, because I want another shot at him, as a matter of fact I think we should question him together. That was we can cover each other from his false accusations."

"Good idea." Hank answered. I'm going to start on that right now, I already did some preliminary calling yesterday. And your day ?"

"Track down the directors to see what kind of info I can get on Florence Goodwyn. Let's touch back mid day."

"You got it." Hank commented as they both reached for their phones.

Hanks first inquiry was with Helen Warren, a very young twenty two year old just out of college. Hank's questions were normal yet probing. After ten minutes he was convinced of her innocence, totally. As she was being dismissed she asked about the possibility of getting a research job with the police dept. Sgt. Conrad was flattered she asked but directed her to the administration offices.

His next appointment was on time. A Norman Holt, obviously the serious type, very straight laced. Suit, tie, glasses and shined shoes. A librarian trainee so to speak interested in Ancient History. Hank pictured a similar type sitting in front of him when he was in high school and laughed to himself.

Question results were the same with him as with Helen Warren. Of course no one was free from suspicion but Hank relegated young Norman to the bottom of the list.

He returned to his office just as his phone was ringing.

"Conrad here."

"Hank, Tommy Grant here. I was one of the uniforms that was with you yesterday."

"Oh right, what can I do for you Tom ?"

"It's the other way around Sarge. It's what I can possibly do for you."

"Okay, you have tweaked my interest, what have you got ?"

"Some thoughts about yesterdays search at the library. My shift ends in about an hour, can I meet with you. I'll only be a few blocks away."

"Sure thing Tom, I'll wait for you."

As the Sgt. hung up the phone curious thoughts ran through his mind. *"What possible information could he have about the library that we don't know. Oh well, I need another coffee."*

Sgt. Mark Dwyer entered a very upscale high rise and was directed to the tenth floor. He was to meet with a Lawrence Metcalf. Mr. Metcalf was chair of the library board of directors.

"Thank you Sir for taking the time from your busy day to meet with me." Mark started.

"Not at all Sergeant. How can I be of help in this terrible tragedy."

Mark gaged Mr. Metcalf to be a highly successful person who also dressed the part.

"Thank you again Sir in advance for your cooperation. We need some background history of the deceased and thought members of the board could help. Information such as residence, friends, relatives, work history and possible enemies. Anything that provides an insight to her background and personality.

"In anticipation of some of your questions I pulled her file and had a copy made for you. We go into great detail in our interviews for these library positions. After all we are dealing with the public at large and must keep a face of true public interest and service."

"Oh brother, this guy must be running for congress." thought Mark

"That sounds like just what we are looking for. On a more personal level, how well did you know Ms. Goodwyn ?"

Not the least bit offended by the question, Metcalf answered directly.

"I did not personally have any social interaction with Florence other than our quarterly meetings. If you check with Mrs. Broadhurst, I believe she was somewhat active socially with Ms. Goodwyn. I'm sure she can provide more insight into her personal life."

"Thank you Mr. Metcalf for your time, I don't think we will have to call on you a second time but- - -"

Dwyer was cut off mid sentence.

"I am at your service day or night Sergeant. I will cooperate in any way I can."

The two men stood and shook hands meaningfully. As Mark turned to go he held up the personnel file on Florence saying "Once again thanks." He checked his watch and decided to go back to headquarters.

~ ~ ~ ~ ~ ~

"Come in Tom, you really have my curiosity running amuck. Fill me in please." pleaded Hank.

"Well after I got home last night I started thinking about the sewage spot on the floor."

"Hold on Tom, this sounds like something perhaps Sgt. Blake should be in on."

Hank grabbed the phone dialing the lab extension.

"Susan can you come to my office. We have something you may be interested in."

Hanging up the phone he turned to Tom; "Give her a few minutes. In the meantime let's get some coffee. I'll even buy."

Six minutes passed and Susan showed at the office door. Introductions were made while they all found a chair. Hank nodded his head for Tom to begin.

"As I stated before, I started thinking about the spots on the floor that Sgt. Blake discovered and it triggered some old memories. An old uncle of mine used to work for the city sewer works. I can still hear my aunt yelling at him to remove his shoes before entering the house. Any way, he used to tell stories of the old sewer system that is not really used anymore, that ran under the whole city with access to a lot of older buildings. Direct access. It has since been blocked off because of the newer, more efficient system. I thought about it being blocked off but after all these years how well could that be. Something that old, unless it is maintained, doesn't last forever."

Hank and Susan were looking at each other, a small grin appearing. The sparkle that showed in their eyes betrayed their active minds.

"If I'm not mistaken the building now housing the library is one of the oldest in the city.

"I'll get right on it." said Susan as she left Hank's office.

"Where is she going ?" asked Tom

Hank still wearing the small grin answered, "The old records files at the Sewer Dept. I imagine."

"You mean this information means something to you."

"You bet it does, Tom. Thanks for being astute enough to make that connection. Dwyer is going to be very happy about this."

"Glad I could be of service." Tom said as he left..

~ ~ ~ ~

Mark could barely contain his excitement on hearing about Tom's story.

"Perhaps other pieces will fall into place now."

"That would be nice but I'm not going to hold my breath." Hank answered.

"How did your interview go ?"

"Well I guess. I did two of the younger staff who were both cooperative. There was nothing from either of them. Frankly I believe both of them innocent. How did you make out with the directors ?"

"I only did the chairman and he was most helpful with leads to other people. I'll continue that tomorrow."

"I'll hit the other two staff people tomorrow morning also. That will still leave me free for most of the day." volunteered Hank.

"We'll check with Blake first thing to see if she discovered anything." Dwyer remarked. How about a beer before we head home ?"

"You're on." Hank smiled in answer.

Day three.

	Nine AM and Hank was already in one of the interview rooms with another of the staff, Ann Jackson. Ann had been with the library for about three years. Her duties were mostly at the front reception desk. A sort of all around person to the other library staff. Obviously very dedicated, she would work or fill in where ever and when ever she was needed. A married woman with three children and led a full life. Her time was portioned fully. Hank, being honest with himself could not see how she could possibly be part of this murder. He did however continue his normal line of questioning so that he would have complete reports for all the staff.

	Just before being dismissed Ann spoke up.

	"Oh, one more thing Sgt. You may learn more from Joyce or Norman. They both were closer to Florence and lately to each other. I don't mean to tell tales but I got the impression in the past few months they might have been sweet on each other. I know Florence was like a mother figure to Joyce."

	"Thank you Miss Jackson for your candor and cooperation. And I must ask you as I do everyone, that what ever words passed between us will stay between us. Please do not discuss our session with anyone else." Mark suggested.

	"By all means Sgt. I fully understand and you can count on my disression."

	Smiling, Hank politely escorted Ann Jackson to the door.

~ ~ ~ ~

	At the same time on the other side of town Dwyer was just entering the office of Janice Broadhurst. Ms. Broadhurst was vice chair of the library board. A pleasant but well disciplined no nonsense woman. She welcomed Sgt. Dwyer with a warm handshake and accompanying smile.

"I spoke with Mr. Metcalf and I think I will be able to fill you in with the details you appear to be looking for."

"Thank you for your cooperation. I know discussions such as this are not always easy and I will try to be brief.

Over the next fifteen minutes Ms. Broadhurst was able to enlighten Mark with many details of Florence Goodwyns life styles. Apparantly well liked by all, she was socially accepted no matter what the group or project was. It appears as if she had no enemies of any sort.

"A rare person indeed." thought Mark. *"Which is really no help. I"m looking for possible answers and I'm running into dead ends."*

Mark ended this interview totally frustrated. He knows nothing more now than when he walked into Ms. Broadhurst's office. He went through the routine of thanking her and exited the building.

On the way back to the station he decided not to pursue any more board members, at least not at this time. Metcalf and Broadhurst more than answered his questions. Of very little help but he thought there was nothing else to uncover.

~ ~ ~ ~ ~ ~

Sgt. Blake suddenly felt like an archeologist discovering a lost tomb as she unfolded blueprint after blueprint of squiggly and zig zag lines. There were off shoots going every which way covered with numbers and various indicator marks. She was intensely pleased because this is why she entered the forensics field. This art of discovery and puzzle solving was like a vitamin tonic to her, or more like an uplifting ecstasy for her.

Once orientated she was able to follow certain routes which she compared with a present day ground map of the city. It took a bit longer than she thought and finally found the common link she was looking for. After that it wasn't too long till she hit the jackpot. "BINGO" she exclaimed out loud. Sure enough there was a tunnel leading right to the library. Checking the index key of symbols she noted, yelled "BINGO" for a second time. There was a stairwell leading to the first floor of the library. Locating a floor plan of the library she was able to narrow it down to the north wall of the building. The rest would have to be checked at the building itself since there had been various changes to the building over the years. Susan was really excited now and was anxious to tell Dwyer and Conrad. Feeling quite proud she secured the maps on her table, locked her lab door and went for a cup of coffee.

~ ~ ~ ~ ~ ~

It was eleven eighteen when Mark's cell phone buzzed.

"Dwyer here"

"Sgt. Dwyer I understand you are the one leading the investigation of that terrible library murder."

"That's correct." he answered.

"My name is Cynthia Hopkins and I am a hostess for Community Airways. I don't have time now, my flight is leaving in ten minutes. I have some information I would like to share with you that may or may not be pertinent. I arrive back here tonight at seven twenty at gate twenty three. Would it be possible for you to meet me. I only have a three hour layover and I'm gone again. I feel it may be important to you."

"You have my utmost interest, Miss Hopkins and yes I will meet you at the airport. I'll be wearing a dark blue suit and light blue tie and I'll make sure I have a white handkerchief in my pocket."

"That will be wonderful and thank you, I have to run now, see you tonight."

Sgt. Dwyer stood there looking at a silent phone. "Who knows, maybe I'll finally get a break." he mumbled aloud to no one. There were no other messages waiting so he made his way to the station house.

~ ~ ~ ~

Sgt. Conrad had a short interval between interviews, just enough time for a cup of coffee. On his way back to the interview room he was notified that Lilly Schmitt had arrived. She was escorted to the waiting Sgt. She looked a bit nervous and uneasy. Hank assured her this was just routine. Lilly told her story of discovering the body along with Joyce. She admitted being sick to her stomach upon seeing the body. She screamed and ran from the area instantly. She did not even know who the victim was until later. She was so upset and shocked that she just ran.

"I think Joyce was in shock also. She just stood there."

Hank let her settle a minute or so before continuing, he even poured her a glass of water.

"How long have you worked at the library ?"

"Not quite two and a half years. I really like it there."

"Did the staff get along together ?"

"Oh yes, very well I think. Joyce seemed to be Florence's pet, I'm sorry I mean Miss Goodwyn. You would think they were related, but then again Joyce has been there the longest."

"What about Norman Holt ? Being the only male staff member did he get along with the rest of you ?"

"Norman's a funny sort. Very straight laced, although the last few months he appeared to be very chummy with Joyce. I don't know why though., she is much older than he is. As far as Flor......, Miss Goodwyn goes it was, I think, a normal work relationship. He was so precise in everything he did. It would be hard to find fault with anything he was involved with, except maybe he could have smiled more."

Lilly said the last with a grin of her own. Turning serious again she inquired quietly;

"Am I going to lose my job because of this ?"

"I wouldn't think so Lilly. The library will be open again soon enough." Hank offered.

Thinking of Twining he added with a smile, "And you do have to serve the public needs."

Lilly was more at ease now that she vented some of her feelings. Hank decided not to push any further now. He could always call her back. He thanked her, gave the usual cautions and walked her to the door.

Hanks mind was immediately working anew. *"That's the second comment regarding Norman Holt and Joyce Lambertson. He might just call Joyce again but that must be discussed with Mark as soon as he returned."*

He entered his office and checked his phone for messages. There were two. The first from Blake wanting the three of them to meet ASAP. The second from Dwyer informing him of the meeting that night with the airline hostess. Hank did manage a return call to Mark and it was agreed to meet at 0800. Hank then called Susan and relayed Mark's message. She was a bit disappointed because she wanted to share her discovery but agreed that the three meet in the morning.

~ ~ ~ ~ ~ ~

Mark's trip to the airport reminded him of why he hates airports. The drive took three times as many minutes as it was in miles from the station. Traffic was horrendous, parking even worse. Than there was the long walk to the building housing Community Airways. Finally locating gate twenty three he checked his watch. He had five minutes to spare. "I guess I should have left earlier." he mumbled.

At seven twenty seven an extremely attractive woman appeared.

"Sgt. Dwyer ?"

"Yes Mam, and you must be Cynthia Hopkins."

"The one and only." she smiled.

Mark's thoughts forgot why he was there for a moment. *"You're almost too good to be true. Down boy, back to work."*

After that short pause Mark returned the smile.

"Is there somewhere quiet we can go to ?"

"Yes , we can go to the crew's lounge. It won't be totally quiet but it will be a lot better then this madhouse."

With that she hooked her arm in his and walked away from the gate area. Three minutes later they entered a relatively quiet room with lockers, lounge chairs and a mini kitchenette. Cynthia directed him to grab a chair as she did and dragged them over to a quiet corner. Cynthia started with.

"Thank you for meeting with me." as they made themselves comfortable.

Getting right to the point the Sgt. tried to stay all business.

"You said you had what might be important information."

"Looking at her is going to make it difficult to concentrate." his thoughts wandered. Mark caught sight of a modest ring which he took as an engagement ring. This helped him put his mind back on track as to why he was here.

"Yes Sgt. It has to do with that Mr. Twining , the library person."

Mark's ears perked right up as did his temperature.

"I saw him on the television during his interview with the media. He spoke of himself as free and clear of any suspicion, no matter what the police thought, and that he had an airtight alibi."

Dwyer could feel himself grow tense just at the mention of that name.

"Yes, I'm aware of our differences of opinion. But go on, how does that have anything to do with our investigation ?"

"Well he said he was on flight 640 to Philadelphia on Friday. I worked that flight and yes there was a Mr. Harold Twining on the passenger list."

She paused a second looking puzzled.

"The man in that flight was not the same one I saw on the TV."

Instant alarms went off in Mark's head. *"Perhaps I am going to get a break for once."*

"Are you certain of that Miss Hopkins ?"

"Yes, I'm quite positive. He was the third person to enter the cabin and it was I who checked his name off. You can check my accuracy by viewing the tapes."

"What tapes ?" Marked asked.

"With the new security measures because of terrorist activity there are closed circuit TV cameras at the entrance gates. Every person entering the aircraft is filmed as they pass through the gate. I hope I'm not out of line with this information, I just thought it might be important."

"You are doing the right thing, I wish there were more civic minded citizens to help the police. Do you know who has these tapes and where I can get to see them ?"

"I guess airport security but ultimately I think the FBI controls them."

Cynthia reached into her travel bag and pulled out a paper handing it to Mark.

"This is the flight number and gate and boarding time for that flight on Friday."

By this time Mark wanted to give her a big hug and thank you for such a great piece of information, though he did remain professional.

"Do you think this could be of any help to your investigation ?" Cynthia inquired.

"It certainly will be Miss Hopkins and I can't thank you enough." Mark answered showing his excitement.

Cynthia was smiling feeling good about herself.

"Well there is one way you can thank me."

"And what would that be ?" asked Mark.

Looking at her watch she answered;

"Well, I still have two hours before my next flight. You could buy me a quick burger or something for my dinner." Self consciously she added, "That is if you have the time. I don't want to interfere with your work."

"A burger it is, lead the way."

Mark felt that he really should not be doing this but then again how bad could it be with hundreds of people around. Cynthia was astute enough not to pursue anything further as far as the investigation. They talked about inconsequential things while eating. Just before parting she handed Mark a paper with her name and address and phone number.

"Just in case you have any further questions for me."

She took his hand saying good bye. "By the way I'm not on call this coming weekend." She smiled, turned and walked away with Mark staring at her till he lost her in the crowd.

"Excuse me Sir." an elderly woman in a walker said.

Mark came out of his spell seeing that the woman wanted to pass.

"I'm sorry Mam." he smiled as he stepped aside then aimed for the exit door.

Traffic was no better on the ride home.

Day four

Mark entered his office, coffee in hand, at seven twenty five only to find Hank already there updating his interview reports. Simultaneously they both started talking about their exciting news. Chuckling Mark said;

"Okay, you first.

Hank took the queue and laid out details of his interviews. Finally stating the fact that two people spoke of Norman and Joyce being close but only recently. "Norman never mentioned a relationship with Joyce during his interview."

"Nor did Joyce when I first spoke with her." Mark interrupted. "Perhaps we should have a second talk with her."

"I was thinking the same thing but I wanted to check with you first." Hank replied. "Blake is very eager that we three meet. She should be here shortly."

"Good, that gives me time to fill you in on last evenings meeting with the airline hostess."

"I'm glad it was you that went to the airport rather than me. It's such a tedious drive and parking is a nightmare." Hank was smiling when he said this because they were the words he heard from Mark many times.

"Next time I'll make sure it's you who goes." Mark chided back. Any how this hostess said Harold Twining was on the flight to Philly, but it was not the one we know."

"Whoa, that's very interesting. Our loud mouth is lying to us."

"It seems that way but I still have to verify Miss Hopkins story, though I do believe her."

"So she was that pretty, was she." kidded Hank.

Mark lightly blushed but went along with the joking.

"I or maybe "WE" have to go back to the airport to view the CCTV tapes."

"Didn't you say you have the contact person in Philadelphia ? A call to him may be in order."

"Naa.... I have a good friend of mine on the Philly PD. I think I can get him to do the legwork for us.'

"Good deal." smiled Hank. "I really didn't want to go to Philly. So when do we put Twining in the hot seat?"

"Let's check the tapes first." Mark commented.

Just then Sgt. Blake poked her head in.

"Am I interrupting anything ?"

"Not at all Susan, pull up a chair."

"I'd rather have you two pull up a chair in my lab."

"Is your news that good." questioned Hank.

"I think so." smiled Susan.

They followed her to the downstairs lab. She unlocked the door flipping the lights on

"Join me at the big table" she invited.

Uncovering her map layout with a big grin she stated, "Gentlemen, I believe we have hit the jackpot."

She gave a quick run down of the different maps ending with her finger on the library stairwell.

"The only thing I haven't worked out yet is the entry point to this underground cavern because of the extent of the city. There are or were many entrances."

"This is fantastic Susan, I could give you a big hug for this."

She blushed thinking to herself, *"What's stopping you."* The moment ended as quickly as it came when Hank volunteered to join that hug. The three were like school kids at the last bell. Finally Mark said.

"Okay let's try and get serious again."

"Party pooper." Susan chided with a big smile.

"This obviously rated a trip to the library. Care to join us Susan, after all it's your brilliant work that got us this far."

"You couldn't keep me away." she replied.

Glancing at the wall clock Mark resumed outlining his thoughts.

"It's just after ten now so we should head right over there. Give me ten minutes to check in and update the Captain. I'll meet you upstairs by the door."

The report to the Captain was brief and Dwyer joined the waiting pair.

Fifteen minutes later found the now trio at the library. The patrolman at the door greeted them with a smile, his job not being very exciting.

"Everything Ok ?" asked Hank.

"All is peace and quiet." was the reply. "Except the Mr. Twining guy was here wanting to get in. He seemed really ticked off that I refused. He said something about I'll hear about this from my superiors."

The three Sgt's laughed.

"Don't let it bother you, we have your back." replied Mark as he unlocked the door.

Once inside the three went to the north wall. Susan pointed out where the mud spots ended. Right in front of a six tiered book shelf. Hank studied it for a moment then with excitement said louder than usual;

"Look here, this thing has got recessed wheels."

Mark and Susan were also grinning as Mark joined Hank at one end.

"No wait ! Susan said with alarm.

The two men turned to her.

"Fingerprints." she smiled

Embarrassed yet acknowledging her attention to detail, each reached into their pocket for their gloves. While in that process she suggested they push, if possible, from someplace that would not be a common handhold. They did as she asked. Without very much effort the nine foot long shelving began to slide.

Again Susan yelled, "Wait. Swing it out toward me as you do that."

Her comment hit Mark and Hank at the same time.

"Oh, right. That makes more sense, a larger opening with less pushing." said Hank. "I guess that's why they pay you the big bucks Susan." he joked.

"You got it, I just have this job to keep boredom from setting in." She chided back.

Suddenly the three were silent. They were looking at an almost hidden door. Lacking a door frame and painted to blend in with the wall it went almost undetected. With the book shelf in front of it. It totally disappeared.

"Look." Susan pointed. "Sewage mud, if there is such a thing."

True enough there were a few traces of the same mud she had obtained previously and tested in the lab.

Hank came up with his pocket knife and with little or no strain the three by four foot door opened. Stale damp air wafted into the large room.

"Ah yes," Mark said. "Nothing like the aroma of well aged sewage."

Flashlight in hand Hank took the first step into the darkened cavity. He was on a metal grid landing that topped a steep, narrow, spiral stair also of metal. Susan was again quick to point out mud residue on the grid. "This is relatively fresh." She stooped down and took a sample for the lab.

Hank continued cautiously down into the darkness. Nearing the bottom he could detect the echo of his steps on the metal. Once on flat ground he could hear the rustle of movement. Twirling around with the light he could see many large rats scurrying away.

"I'm on solid ground now." he called up. "I think there are about twenty steps. We are definitely well under the city."

Susan right away started down before Mark could stop her. She still considered this the discovery part and was thrilled with the excitement it generated in her. Mark was close on her heels.

"Okay, now we know how the killer entered the library without a key but how do you enter this maze of tunnels ?" He turned to Susan for an answer.

"I have yet to finish deciphering all the symbols but I would safely venture to say there are well over a hundred access ports."

"Oh great!" Mark sighed. "Any other good news ?"

Blake confidently answered in the positive. "I would also be willing to bet that most have been permanently sealed off. I will continue to work on the schematics to identify them all. It will take some time but I will do it." she smiled positively.

"How about Tom Grant." Hank volunteered.

"What about him ?" Mark asked.

"I don't know, I just thought that he had a familiarity with the sewer system perhaps he or even his uncle could be of assistance."

"You're right. That's a great idea. I never turn down a chance to learn something new." bubbled Sgt. Blake.

"Okay, we'll see if we can get him temporarily assigned to Blake." Mark decided. "Let's hope his uncle is still alive, I don't know of any old timers left at the sewer department."

They all agreed there was nothing else they could do that would be of any consequence at this time.

Re-securing the door and bookcase they were about to leave when Sgt. Blake realized they had sewage residue on their shoes. She mentioned this which set off bells for Mark and Hank.

"We can't check the public but we can check on the staff.. Of course we will need a court order. Hank suggested.

"I'll see the Captain as soon as we get back to the station." Mark offered. "And you young lady have done it again. Thanks for your help. Perhaps you could get a transfer to the detective squad."

"No thanks." Susan answered. "I love my work in forensics and that's where I want to stay."

"Maybe you're right, this way you get to help us all."
Susan proudly smiled again.

~ ~ ~ ~

"I'm sure we can get the DA to help us with a court order but that certainly is not going to help our case with Twining." the Captain stated.

"I know that Sir and I am hoping we can count on you again to keep him at arms length. I believe we are slowly making some progress and I don't want it fouled up now." explained Dwyer.

"You still have my backing Sgt. Let's get this thing ended."

"Thank you Sir. Oh, and one other thing. Sgt. Blake has been of great help. I believe she should get the recognition she deserves."

"I will see to that also Sgt. replied the Captain as he reached for his ringing phone and indicated for Mark to leave.

~ ~ ~ ~

The two key people left to re-interview are Twining and Lambertson. But I would rather wait till after we get our court order and do the shoe check." Dwyer remarked. Continuing he said. "I'll let you do whatever you think is necessary, I'm going to the airport again to explore the CCTV tapes.

"Lucky you." smiled Hank. "Have fun and keep me posted. I can always work with Susan for a while."

Mark grabbed his coat and disappeared out the door.

~ ~ ~ ~

Sgt. Dwyer took a deep breath walking from the parking lot to the security office. He didn't know why he always let traffic get to him, he was usually so patient. He found security and after identification verification was completed he was ushered to the tape room. Having the day, time and flight number made it easy to locate the tape in question. A security man played the tape for him pausing it at Mark's request. Sure enough there was Cynthia Hopkins and the third passenger to enter the boarding tunnel at the gate. And she was correct, that was not Harold Twining. There was no second guessing. It was a view full face and unmistakable. Mark could feel his excitement factor rise about twenty points.

The people there were most cooperative and made copies for him while he waited. He thanked them profusely and couldn't wait to get back to the office and transmit it to his contact in Philadelphia. Mark was on such a high returning to the office he hardly noticed the traffic.

~ ~ ~ ~

Looking at Mark's glowing face, Hank knew it had been a successful afternoon for him. He also had a fruitful day with Susan. Tom spent the afternoon with them along with another retired old timer, who was thrilled that he could be of help interpreting the old maps. Tom's uncle had passed away but this was a co worker from the old sewer works. Feeling that they were finally making progress they called it quits for the day. Hank quietly said "See you tomorrow." with a quick wave of his hand.

Mark shut down his computer and was about to leave himself when he saw the paper Cynthia gave him with her address and phone number. He hesitated for a moment then told himself, why not. "I'll just pretend its in the line of duty." He laughed lightly to himself. Successfully getting through to her he made arrangements to meet her at the airport Saturday evening after her last flight at seven thirty five. That should make for an interesting night he said with a smile. He killed the lights in his office and departed thinking of what he was going to have for supper.

Day five.

Much to their surprise by mid morning they had the court order in hand. For the search of six residences to check for mud residue on shoes.

"Tell you what." Mark posed. "Let me first check to see if my Pal in Philly made contact yet. Then you take a team to see Norman Holt and Ann Jackson. I'll take another team and do Lilly Schmit and Helen Warren. We will leave Twinning till I hear from Philly and will do him together."

"And Joyce Lambertson ?" asked Hank.

"I think we'll do her together also. We'll give her a little more time to recover from her shock of finding the body. I was just thinking of this Joyce - Norman thing. Perhaps it's merely an ordinary office romance thing that they are trying to keep private."

"I suppose it could be." answered Hank. "We'll find out soon enough.'

Dwyers Philly pal was still working on the Twining ID and promised to have the answer by late afternoon. Mark and Hank went their separate ways to check the staff shoes for mud residue. Mark had no problem finding Lilly and Helen home and most cooperative. Results were negative for each.

In the meantime Hank, a fair distance away, called upon Ann Jackson. She was surprised and confused at the request but showed no hesitation in allowing the team to check all her shoes. Hank also drew a blank as far as the residue in question.

Next stop Norman Holt in another part of town. There was no answer. Hank sought out the super of the building only to be told Norman had not been seen for two days. But then again the super admitted not being around much in those two days. Without too much coaxing the super agreed to open the apartment. He was asked to wait outside while the team performed a thorough search. The apartment was spotless with everything as neat as a pin. Even the magazines were neatly piled according to size. The whole place reflected how his co-workers described him. A pair of upscale tennis shoes, lined up with other foot wear like soldiers at inspection, yielded the results Hank was looking for. Mud traces that, to his eyes, looked the same as the sample that Susan had been studying. He had a sample taken for Susan's further studies.

There was no sign of a hurried departure, in fact suitcases and over night bags were tucked away as if there for quite a spell.

Slightly but not overly concerned Hank and his team left everything exactly as they found it and departed. Hank noted to himself to check with this Norman Holt later in the day or call this evening. He also wanted to get the lab results on the mud before he thought of any formal accusations.

~ ~ ~ ~

Returning to police headquarters Hank went immediately to the lab. Susan accepted the sample and promised to work on it right away.

Dwyer was in the office with his feet up, sipping his coffee when Hank joined him. He perked up right away upon hearing of Norman's shoes and was equally upset that Norman may be missing.

Forty minutes later Susan joined the two men, report in hand.

"It's a perfect match." she announced excitedly.

"Based on that." Mark posed to get a man to his apartment ASAP. Keep a twenty four hour stake out there until Mr. Holt shows. He may be involved but I still have a gut feel this was more than a one person job.

Sgt. Blake also spoke of her day with Tom Grant and an old timer recruited by Tom who really knows the old system well.

"As I thought." Susan posed, "Many of the entrances have been permanently sealed or have been done away with completely. Ron, That's the old timer, has been most helpful. He appears to know the whole tunnel system like his own name. He has narrowed it down for us to about twenty possibilities. What we now have to do is make on site inspections of those possibilities. Above ground and underground. Which reminds me when we do start the physical search I will put a fingerprint team on the hidden door and landing and those curvy stairs."

"You do cover all the bases don't you." commented Mark.

With her usual smile Susan answered, "I try Mark, I try." She then continued after her own interruption. "Tom and myself along with two uniforms volunteers will start the search tomorrow. We will start the closest to the library first and work our way out."

"Do you have all the necessary equipment?" inquired Mark.

"I believe so, even down to portable oxygen masks if needed. As I said Ron has been most helpful."

"Is Ron going with you ?" Hank asked.

Susan smiled answering, "He wants to but admits himself at eighty three years old his body just isn't up to it any more. But we will be in touch by radio if any questions come up.

"I should think not, but he obviously has been of great assistance. We'll have to figure a way to thank him." said Mark.

"The thrill of just being useful again was its own reward as far as he is concerned, but you are right. Recognition of some kind would be appropriate

"It feels good to finally be making progress, as little as it may seem." Mark said generalizing. "We have to wait now for my Philly friend. To come through. If he verifies what Cynthia Hopkins says we'll get him in tomorrow for a thorough grilling. It appears there is no need for all three of us to be here this afternoon so why don't you two make it an early day. Tomorrow we can start fresh. I'll report to the Captain then wait for Philly." suggested Mark.

There was no argument from either Susan or Hank. Soon Mark was on his way to the Captain

~~~~

The meeting with Captain Braddick was brief yet he did appear to be pleased with the results so far. Mark went back to his office to await the call from Philadelphia. He reviewed everything to date in his mind. Two tentative suspects stood out, Harold Twining and Norman Holt. Of course that does not consider outsiders which is always a possibility. But even with suspects, what
~~~~

motive is behind such a brutal murder. His thoughts were getting him no where and he could feel himself drifting to sleep. Rather than give in he went to the coffee machine.

It was five thirty and two coffees past when the phone rang.

"Dwyer here." was Mark's quick answer. "Woody, it's good to hear your voice again. It's been a long time. Regards to the wife and kids. So what do you have for me? You have confirmed the picture I sent you. Great news ! I hope I didn't put you out too much. Did you ask if he went under the name of Twining ?"

"No, he used his own name. He said he was representing Twining though there was no transaction. Twining's man didn't think the book was worth it."

"What name did he go by."

"George Harper, you'll have to get addresses from your Twining fellow."

"I can't thank you enough Woody. This means a lot to me. I owe you one. Thanks again."

Mark hung up smiling. "Gotcha" he exclaimed out loud. He knew this did not make it a sure thing but it was enough to recall Harold Twining for a second chat.

He went right to the Captain with this new information and caught him as he was leaving. Braddick patiently listened and even agreed to call Twining to avoid confrontation before the interview even started.

Mark finally felt satisfied enough to call it a day. He went home to relax.

Day six.

Still feeling good because of his friend's news last night Mark was back in his office by seven AM. He couldn't wait for Hank to show to share the breakthrough.

Hank entered the shared office a few minutes after eight. He told Mark how well rested he was and was raring to go. Gazing at Mark's face he knew something was up.

"You heard from your Pal, didn't you ?" he stated.

"You bet I did. We now have proof Twining lied to us." Mark replied smiling. "The Captain has already been informed and to make sure Mr. Harold Twining didn't balk by us calling him, The Captain called himself. Our Mr. Importance is scheduled to be here at ten thirty. You and I can then have the pleasure of talking to him."

"I think I'm going to enjoy our little chat." said Sgt. Conrad.

Off to the coffee machine to have a celebratory drink. Susan Blake met them there and joined in their toast. She outlined her planned day for Mark and Hank. Tom Grant was already securing the necessary equipment.

The trio went back to the lab and were introduced to Ron. Both were surprised at how alert and agile this eighty three year old was. He looked fit enough to go down to the tunnels but Mark was pleased the old man had sense enough to know his own limitations. Susan excused herself and her team and headed for the sewer tunnels.

Dwyer and Conrad went back to their office to review and list questions for the up coming interview. At ten twenty the pair made their way to the interrogation room. Conrad checked the tape machine to ensure proper function and Mark checked that the water jug was filled and chilled.

At ten thirty five as promised Capt. Braddick delivered Harold Twining to the waiting Sergeants. As the Captain opened the door and stepped aside to allow Mr. Twining entrance, Harold instantly saw Dwyer and Conrad.

"These gentlemen have some questions for you Sir. Your cooperation would be greatly appreciated."

The sight of the two Sgts. naturally triggered an instant response from Harold.

"Hey ! What is this ? Captain you indicated you wanted to see me."

"That is correct Mr. Twining and these two gentlemen will be asking questions in my stead."

With that Braddick turned away and closed the door.

"Please have a seat and make yourself comfortable Mr. Twining." Mark asked with a smile and as pleasant a voice as he could muster.

"I don't understand. Why am I here." Harold spoke in a haughty voice. "I already gave you my statement."

"That is correct Sir." commented Sgt. Conrad. "And it is that statement we want to discuss."

"Your supervisors will hear about this." Twining said in a very loud and indignant voice.

"You are right Sir, and we will tell them ourselves."

This statement stopped Twining ranting and changed his expression.

"Now if you please Mr. Twining have a seat and we can begin." Mark said calmly. "And for the record and your own security this meeting will be recorded."

Hank started the tape rolling and made the starting entry.

"October nine, two thousand sixteen. Interview with Harold Twining conducted by Sgt. Mark Dwyer and Sgt. Hank Conrad. Starting time is ten forty five.

Harold sat down visibly disturbed. It was yet to be determined whether it was fear, arrogance or disbelief.

"For the record Sir would you state your name and address." Mark asked.

"Harold Twining." He spoke loud and clear and after giving his address he questioned;

"Don't I have the right to an attorney ?"

"That is your right Sir and if you wish you may call one from here. But be advised we will hold you here until he arrives." stated Mark.

This sort of set him aback. The expression on his face was now a mix of uncertainty and confusion. The room was quiet for a few moments, Twining obviously deep in thought. He looked at the tape machine as if he were addressing it and calmly spoke,

"As I explained earlier I already gave you my statement."

"I agree that you did give a statement Mr. Twining. What we are trying to establish now is perhaps you want to amend that statement." Mark asked professionally

"Why would I want to do that." Harold answered with a smirk.

Hank, also composed and professional asked;

"Where were you this past weekend."

With a quiet laugh he answered.

"I already told you I was in Philadelphia on business."

"Can you prove that ?" Mark furthered.

"Of course I can, I told you that also."

Now Harold Twining was sporting a large "I Gotcha" smile. He then sat down as smug as can be.

Hank then quietly asked;

"Then who is George Harper ?"

Twining's face fell. Now looking at both men in disbelief, his expression gave him away.

"Why, I have no idea what you're talking about." he stuttered in reply.

"I think you do, Mr. Twining." Mark said softly. You know with holding information from the police is one thing, and may not seem much to you, but when it interferes with a murder investigation it is a whole other matter."

"So, if you don't mind ?" Hank asked again, "Who is George Harper ?"

"You tell me since you seem to know already. I have no idea who he is." Harold commented yet with his smug attitude.

"Okay, Mr. Twining, we will do just that." Hank continued calmly with no facial expression of any kind. "This Mr. George Harper is the one who flew to Philadelphia in your place. He was in your assigned seat, and boarded the aircraft using your ticket under your name. Why is that so, Mr. Twining ? Did you lose your ticket and this George Harper found it. I don't think so, although you do look somewhat alike."

By now Harold was sweating along with shaking hands while trying to drink water. He avoided eye contact.

"Oh yes, I almost forgot, your contact in Philly spoke with George Harper, Not Harold Twining."

"That's preposterous." Harold yelled out. "You're just making this all up to confuse me and get me to say things about something I know nothing of. In fact I think I changed my mind. I do want to call my lawyer. These accusations have just got to stop."

"Very well Mr. Twining, that is your privilege." Looking over to Hank with an extremely serious face Mark continued with; "Sgt. Conrad, see that arrangements are made for Mr. Twining to contact his Attorney. In the meantime book him on suspicion of murder and withholding evidence during a murder investigation. When you finish with the paper work lock him up. In the meantime I will go see the Captain and the D.A. Have a better day Mr. Twining."

Sgt. Dwyer stood and headed for the door. As Hank produced a set of hand cuffs he asked Harold to stand.

With panic and urgency in his voice Harold protested vehemently.

"No, wait ! Please don't do this. I am innocent. I did not kill Miss Goodwyn. Please don't do this."

Mark stopped with his hand on the door. Turning slowly he asked.

"Can you prove that you didn't do it."

Red faced and severe panic in his eyes he managed to say;

"Yes I can and please listen to me. What I am about to say must not go beyond this room. Please promise me that."

"We don't usually make that sort of promise." said Hank.

Before he even finished speaking Harold interrupted.

"Please I beg of you. I will be admitting something else but it is not murder."

"Okay, Mr. Twining, you have our attention, but we can't promise fully until we hear what you have to say."

Twining's eyes shifted to the tape recorder. Mark nodded to Hank who spoke.

"Interview being temporarily suspended. Time eleven O seven." Hank switched off the recorder.

Slight relief was evident on Harold's face as he returned to his seat. He took another sip of water his hands still shaking. The two Sergeants sat down.

~ ~ ~ ~ ~ ~

Sgt. Blake and her team were well on their way to locating possible entrance points to the tunnel system aside from the library. Ron's memory and preliminary map reviews were right on target. Susan and Tom split up to go in different directions. Each had two other team members. They checked all possibilities, even those that had been permanently sealed. Almost an hour had passed when Susan received a call on her radio.

"Sgt. Blake, this is Tom. I don't mean to interrupt your search but there is something here you just have to see. I'll leave my radio on so you can track my GPS signal to my location.

"Can't you just tell me Tom." said Susan slightly annoyed.

"Please, you have got to see this for yourself."

With a sigh of frustration she answered.

"Okay, I'm on my way."

"What could be that important to interrupt our work, especially down in this sewer?" She asked herself.

It was roughly six minutes before she reached Tom working her way slowly through this intricate maze of tunnels. Upon arrival she started to say straight away:

"Okay, Tom what's so bloody import----.

She froze in place. She was staring at a body wired by the neck and hands to metal piping on the wall. Her bright spot light aimed at the face, which was difficult to make out. A plastic bag was over the head secured tightly around the neck. Suffocation being the obvious cause of death. Susan finally recognized the distorted face as she muttered aloud,

"This is one of the library staff., Norman something or other. Turning to one of her uniformed volunteers with her she calmly ordered;

"Go topside. Notify the ME right away and tell him of this find. Ask him to get his team here ASAP. Then notify Sgt. Dwyer and let him know I will stay on the scene and do my regular job.

Then wait topside at the entrance to guide everyone down.

She was answered with a short yes Sgt. As the man was off and running.

"Nice going Tom, but let's not let this stop our search. I'll stay here with Tony." indicating her other volunteer, while you continue checking the maps. This is going to be more than a one day job."

"Will do." replied Tom.

He was just as glad to get away from this bizarre scene.

Waiting for Dr. Johanson, Susan did some preliminary examination without touching the body. It appeared to be the same type of wire and obviously the same technique of hanging.

"How do you handle such a task." she thought. *"Either you had to be very strong or have an accomplice."* She saw no outward signs of bruising or any indication of a struggle. The rest she would have to leave up to Johanson.

"Dwyer is going to be thrown for a loop with this one." Susan commented to the patrolman with her. All we can do now is wait."

~ ~ ~ ~ ~ ~

Harold's eyes were staring at his feet now as he began to speak.

"You're right, I do know George Harper. He's sort of a friend of mine. We became acquainted a few years back through similar interests. We both collected old first editions. George is actually more knowledgeable than I when it comes to certain authors.

"Is that why he went to Philly instead of you ?" Dwyer asked.

"Well yes and no."

"What do you mean, yes and no ?" inquired Mark "And if he went to Philadelphia for three days what were you doing ? Did this have anything to do with the murder of Florence Goodwyn ?"

"No, not at all. You have to believe me."

Mark pushed further; "Help us believe you. Tell us what you were doing that whole weekend."

"I really can't say right now." Harold mumbled.

"Can't or wont ?   Why, are you protecting someone ? Perhaps the murderer ? Hank quizzed.

No, no, it's not like that. I keep telling you. I had nothing to do with the death of poor Florence."

Harold was starting to show signs of emotional distress again. His body was a jumble of nervous movement.

"Then answer the question, Mr. Twining. Where were you all weekend ?"

Harold took another sip of water but remained silent.

"Look, Harold." said Sgt. Dwyer starting to lose his patience. "You asked us to trust you and I think we have come more than half way. If you want our cooperation then we must have yours. So what's it going to be. Talk to us or we book you for murder."

Appearing upset again, Harold, with his head down mumbled I was with a woman all weekend."

Half smiling Mark replied with;

"And what's wrong with that ?"

There was a long pause again.

"The woman I'm involved with is married."

"Okay, so you're having an affair with another man's wife." Mark said matter of factly. "That's not a new thing in this world. It happens all the time. It's only ------. Mark stopped himself. "Oh I get it. You're having an affair with George Harper's wife. That's why you sent him away for the weekend. Is that correct, Harold.

Yes." he mumbled almost incoherently.

"Can and will she corroborate that ?"

Harold snapped his head around quickly staring directly into Mark's eyes.

"No, you can't do that." He said rather loud. "Please." he pleaded further.

"It seems to me you don't have a choice Mr. Twining. You are facing a serious charge of murder, that is unless you can prove otherwise."

The room became silent. Mark and Hank exchanged glances and almost imperceptible smiles. Five minutes of quiet followed.

Allowing the time to pass Sgt. Dwyer spoke again quietly.

"Tell you what Harold, I am willing to make a deal with you."

Twining slowly looked up showing his interest.

"As you saw the recorder is already off. If you allow us, more for your own benefit, to talk to Mrs. Harper to validate what you have already told us, I promise you it will never leave this room. I am more interested in solving a disturbing murder then prying into or judging another mans behavior. I'll leave your behavior up to your own conscience."

You could tell Harold's mind was working overtime and suddenly the visible tension in his face and body appeared to slowly dissipate. Dwyer gave him a few minutes then asked;

"Do we have a deal Mr. Twining ?"

Harold looked at them both a hint of a question in his eyes.

"You have my word on that, I promise." Mark offered.

Hank followed suit. "And mine." he indicated with a nod of his head.

Another slight pause then a quiet "Yes, we have a deal. How do we go about this ?"

"Well, to keep everything honest and above board without you tipping off your lady friend, can you arrange to meet her somewhere. Then we can ask our questions. We will do it as tenderly as possible without casting aspersions or judgement. If we get a satisfactory answer you will be free to go, no further questions and with nothing on the record."

Checking the wall clock Harold asked to use the phone.

"I'll call her right now and see what I can arrange. Will that be satisfactory ?"

"That will be just fine Mr. Twining, the sooner the better." smiled Dwyer.

Hank pushed the phone across the table.

A tap on the door before it opened allowed the desk Sgt. entry.

"Sorry to but in but can I talk to one of you. It's rather important."

Conrad waved a hand at Mark, "I'll take it." and exited.

~ ~ ~ ~

As the door closed the desk Sgt. began.

"We just had a call from Sgt, Blake's team. They found the body of Norman the librarian. It was hung by wire down in the sewer

-46-

tunnel."

Hank's face drained of color.

"Oh, great. Just what we need, more complexity to an already confusing situation."

"Blake's message indicated that Johanson has been notified and is probably on the scene by now.."

"Thanks Bob, I'll fill Dwyer in."

Hank returned to the interrogation room. Apparently Twinning was finished talking to Mrs. Harper.

"Good, you're back. We're all set, we're leaving now to meet Harold's lady at The Coffee Stop."

Hank drew Mark aside and relayed Blake's message.

"Wonderful." said Dwyer with a purely disgusted look. "Okay, you follow that up, I'll meet you later."

Hank stood aside as Mark and Harold Twining left.

~ ~ ~ ~ ~ ~

It took some time for Hank to make his way to the spot where Norman Holt was found. The body had already been removed by Dr. Johanson's team and was on its way to the lab for post mortem. Sgt. Susan Blake was there waiting for Conrad.

"Where is Dwyer ?" she inquired. Hank ran through a quick explanation of Mark following up a lead without divulging the confidence with Harold Twining. Susan explained the scene as Tom had found it and mentioned that loads of pictures had been taken. They can be reviewed once back at the lab.

"How about you, any luck ?" Hank asked Susan.

"Not yet, we were slowly making progress when the body was found. That really slowed things down. We did, however, eliminate quite a few passageways. Tom and I both agreed we will hit it again tomorrow."

"There goes your weekend." quipped Hank.

"That's alright. Right now I feel this is more important. Especially after today and finding Norman."

~ ~ ~ ~

It was mid afternoon when Hank took his leave from the sewer and made straight for headquarters. Mark had not returned yet so Conrad headed for Johanson's lab.

"I'm not quite finished my exam yet but you can look at the photos.
They are already set up on my computer.

Hank did just that carefully studying each one.
"Just like the Goodwyn woman." he thought. "The wire ?" he casually inquired of the Doctor.

"It looks the same but I'll leave that up to Blake. She's the expert at forensics."

With nothing more to be learned, at least for now, Hank returned to his own office. Mark had also returned. Each shared their reports with the other. Mark ended his with, "I really do believe he is clean now." referring of course to Harold Twining. "At least we will not have any more trouble from him. I think we have made a friend for life."

"That could be both good and bad." laughed Hank. "Not much more to do tonight so I'm going home to a nice hot meal. Care to join me ?"

"Thanks again, but I have plans for tonight." Mark replied. His head still buried in his notes.

"I won't even ask." Hank joked. "See you in the AM."

Mark finished up, and started for the airport with his mind thinking good thoughts for the evening.

Arriving at the designated gate of Community Airways, Mark waited for disembarkment, knowing that the hostesses were usually last. The aircraft emptied but no Cynthia. At last two other hostesses came down the ramp. Mark approached and politely asked about Cynthia Hopkins.

"We would like to know that also." Answered one of the women. "We haven't seen her for three days. All our schedules were thrown off."

Mark stared in disbelief. "I just spoke to her on Wednesday night."

"I'm sorry sir. As I said we would like to know also. She has not answered her phone. I hope she's okay. If I may Sgt. she has been acting rather strange since Wednesday. She had a talk with another woman that morning just before our flight. We asked if she was okay and she said she was fine. Just heard some bad news about a cousin's passing. The last time we saw her was Wednesday evening when she was talking to you. Is everything okay ?"

"I hope so." Mark answered as he walked away, saying thank you over his shoulder. *"I'll call her home again."* He thought.

He left with his mind going wild. By the time he reached home it was almost nine PM. He rang her number, still no answer. There was not much else he could do that night. He would follow up in the morning. He went to bed disappointed about the evening.

Day seven

Mark was up early after an extremely restless night. As his restless night wore on his concern for Cynthia Hopkins grew. Deciding to pick up breakfast on the way he set his course direct for police headquarters. While washing down his egg sandwich with coffee, Hank showed. He was also early. Surprised at each other for being early and on a Sunday, their excuses matched each other. Too many things unanswered were playing havoc with their normal brain routine. They reviewed everything about the case up till then.

At this point Dr. Johanson entered the office.

"Regarding Norman Holt, I thought you two might want to know this. Just as the Goodwyn woman, he was drugged with the same drug. This time it might have been even a larger dose. I have to run now, I'll let you two play with that for a while."

"So it appears to be the same person." commented Mark.

"At least it narrows it down for us." Hank posed.

"How do you narrow down nothing." Mark threw back with a grin. "Joyce is the only staff member left that we have not re - interviewed" he added.

"You're right." replied Mark. "Why don't you follow up on that for now. I have some more CCTV tapes to scan."

"Something new come up ?"

"I'm not sure yet. More like following a hunch. I want to head to the airport right now. Let's say we meet back here by early afternoon. You should be finished with Ms. Lambertson by then. We already know Susan is going sewer diving this morning. We can touch back with her later also."

"Sounds like a plan." Hank agreed. "Joyce should be over her shock by now."

Mark tried Cynthia's number once more with his fingers crossed. There was still no answer.

Both gave their agreed on destinations to the desk Sgt. And each went his own way.

~~~~~~~

Sgt. Susan Blake and officer Tom Grant, maps in hand, were entering the dark, dank tunnels for a third time in three days. It was not yet eight AM. They were hoping to finish early to allow for some free time. That was not to be. At the far end of the city limits their days plan changed drastically. Turning to a short dead end spur their eyes met another mind boggling sight. A very attractive woman wired to wall pipes exactly as Norman Holt. Sgt. Blake knew by the looks of the body that she had there approximately two to three days. Again a plastic bag covering the head secured at the neck . What was once a beautiful face was now a distortion of pain.

Recovering from their initial shock and having notified the ME team, Susan and Tom continued their search for unknown access portals to this underground complex. Their persistence paid off. A metal exit ladder was spotted. It had obviously been used recently. Their spirits soared. They felt their diligence finally gave them results.

Tom climbed the steps to find himself in the basement of an old foundation. Following the muddied foot prints he spotted on the floor brought him to a stair well to an outside yard. It was an old storage bay for the city sewer system filled with both new and old pipes and other necessary equipment for the maintenance of both the water and sewer entities.

Officer Grant returned to report to Sgt. Blake. Some advanced members of the ME team were already on the scene. Susan was elated with Tom's findings. She marked her maps accordingly and was now anxious to get to her lab and the master chart.

Other personnel now took over the crime scene which allowed she and Tom to leave. They were back in the lab just after noon.
~~~~~~~

~ ~ ~ ~ ~ ~

Dwyer found the early Sunday morning traffic a bit easier to cope with and wasn't totally uptight when he arrived at the airport security office. As the last time they were most cooperative. They found Mark a comfortable corner and he reviewed the tapes for Community Airways starting Tuesday morning. He remembered the hostess said Wednesday morning but just to be thorough he chose Tuesday AM to begin.

Luckily there were only nine flights for Community Airways on Tuesday and Sgt. Dwyer reviewed the tapes slowly and meticulously as he could. He gave his eyes a break and accepted the mug of coffee offered before starting on Wednesday's tapes. Two early flights revealed nothing. The next tape to view was just about the time Cynthia called. Twenty minutes before to be exact. Sure enough there was Cynthia at the podium by the gate, clipboard in hand. A woman approached and from Cynthia's big smile, she was obviously known. In their conversation together the other woman's face was now clear for the camera. Mark hit the pause button freezing the frame on Joyce Lambertson. Making note of the reel number, day, time and frame number he went on to play more frames in slow motion. There was no doubt it his mind. It was definitely Joyce. It was not necessary but Mark viewed the tape of the other two following flights netting no new results.

The copies he requested were completed within twenty minutes and a satisfied Mark made a bee line for headquarters.

On the ride back he answered a call from Susan. She outlined what they had found and the fact it was the same method. She herself was on her way to the lab. They could meet later. Mark pondered Susan's call and instantly thought of Cynthia. He hoped he was wrong but deep inside knew that it was. That would be the first thing to check on return to headquarters.

~ ~ ~ ~ ~ ~

After traveling cross town Hank found himself at a fairly

modern hi-rise complex. He counted fifteen stories with two high end restaurants occupying the ground floor. He checked his notes to see that he had the right address for Joyce Lambertson. It was the correct one alright.

"Quite impressive digs for one on a librarians pay." he thought. *"Who knows, perhaps she has a rich uncle."*

Taking the elevator to the eleventh floor, he entered into a plush waiting foyer lavishly appointed with only two doors. The number in his notes indicated the apartment to his left. He rang the bell and gazed around the foyer at the wonderful artwork. Copies, of course, but nevertheless tastefully done. He tried the bell a second time. Not receiving a reply he gave a knock. A second knock netted the same results, nothing. He turned to the elevator about to push the down button when the door quietly opened. A well dressed woman exited with a hello smile.

"Excuse me." Hank started.   "Do you know if Ms. Lambertson is home, I'm not getting an answer."

"She went out earlier, in fact we rode the elevator down together. A lovely woman."

"Okay, thanks, I'll try again later."

"Can I tell her who's calling ?" inquired the woman.

"Just a friend." Hank responded through the closing elevator doors.

In the main lobby Hank checked the resident listings. Landlord ? Super - basement apartment.

A small framed, grey haired woman in her early sixties answered his first knock.

Hank identified himself asking about Joyce.

"Oh my, she's not in any trouble is she ? She's such a kind and caring young lady.."

"Oh no." Hank replied politely. I just wanted to talk to her."

"Oh good." commented the older woman. "Did I tell you how caring she was. She was always so helpful. If she saw me with something heavy, she would always carry it for me. During bad weather she would run to the store for me. A few times she slipped and called me mom. It made me feel so good. Apparently she liked to walk in the park a lot."

Hank's ears perked up.

"She sometimes returned with muddy feet. But she's so

considerate though she always scrubbed then clean before going to her apartment. Right over there by the slop sink. I couldn't ask for a better tenant. A pretty young thing too. I bet she's got a dozen boyfriends, although I've only seen her with one young man recently."

Hank listened patiently wondering when the woman was going to shut up. He took advantage of a short pause.

"How convenient to have this here." he said while drifting towards the large square sink. She may have scrubbed her footwear clean but she did leave mud remnants on the surrounding floor. Hank managed to scrape some samples. He now wanted to get them to the lab for Sgt. Blake to do her thing.

"See what I mean." said the mild mannered super. She always cleans her shoes, She even sweeps the floor sometimes. She is so helpful. You know come tom think of it, maybe it's not the park. She did tell me she volunteered at the Botanical Gardens. Yes, that's must be it."

Hank still smiling politely managed to speak.

"I do have to run now, I'll try her again later. By the way, if you do happen to see her please do not tell her I was here. I would like to keep my visit a surprise."

Looking directly at Hank the woman answered with a smile.

"I understand young man. Mums the word. You can count on me.

Sgt. Conrad believed her and took his leave thanking her profusely.

Finally making it to the outside he was also glad he did not run into Ms. Lambertson. The lab was the only thing on his mind now.

~ ~ ~ ~ ~ ~

Susan Blake was busy with Tom Grant putting the final touches on the city sewer maps of the possible entrance ways when Hank Conrad rushed into the lab with his mud scrapings. He explained where he found them and she promised to do the identification test and comparisons right away.

"I'll be in my office with Mark." he said as he left.

~ ~ ~ ~

Mark and Hank discussed their day's results over fresh coffee, when the ME joined them. Mark had earlier confirmed the third body as Cynthia Hopkins. Johanson's rushed autopsy again found the same drug as the first two deaths. All three murders were basically the same method. The Doctor gave his preliminary findings and returned to his lab. Mark was pleased with today's results yet also had an uneasy feeling. He knew it was Cynthia's death but he realized he had to be the professional and keep going with the case. Hank was much more positive.

"I think it all fits in." commented Hank. "Number one, you have proof Joyce Lambertson spoke with Cynthia Hopkins just before she called you to try and put the blame on Twining. Number two, the method for all three deaths was exactly the same. Number three, all three had connection to the library, one way or another. Number four, Joyce is the only one we have not re interviewed yet. Number five, I know we have to wait for Blake's results on the mud sample but I believe it's the same. Everything points to Ms. Lambertson."

"I know." pondered Mark, "and I agree. What bothers me is , so far we can not come up with a clear motive. You're right though, I guess we will both pay a visit to Ms. Lambertson as soon as we hear from Susan. In the meantime I'll give the Captain a quick rundown. Why don't you get a stake out team on her apartment. Get copies of her picture to that team. If she attempts to leave have her picked up.

Twenty minutes later both were back in the small office patiently waiting. At last Susan showed. She spoke immediately upon entering;

"Your mud sample matched perfectly Hank."

Mark and Hank looked to each other and smiled.

"One more thing that might please you." Susan paused. "That final entrance to the tunnel system we found turned out to be only two short blocks from Lambertson's address. Access would be quite easy and most likely unnoticeable if one was careful."

"That answers number five." Hank voiced.

Without further hesitation Mark stated;

"Okay, let's pick her up. This should be interesting. Care to join us Susan. I know you don't usually get to be in on the finish, but since we owe you so much because of your diligence I thought you might find it rewarding."

Susan, with a happy smile replied instantly;

"I think I would like that Mark. I think it would be inspiring to see the results of one's work."

"Okay, then let's move out." Stated a very enthusiastic Hank.. I'll fill in the desk sergeant and meet you in the parking lot.

The time was now four ten PM.

~ ~ ~ ~ ~ ~

The three Sgt's. were in one car followed by a second un marked car with two plain clothes officers. Upon arrival one officer was posted at the street entrance lobby. The remaining four ascended to the eleventh floor.

The door was answered on the first ring. Joyce Lambertson greeted with a smile. Three entered leaving the lone officer to occupy the foyer area.

"I was expecting you, but I didn't think it would be this soon." said Joyce still wearing a smile. Looking directly at Susan she followed with;

"Men are so stupid. It's nice to see a woman on the team. That's probably why it only took a week to find me."

Sgt's Dwyer and Conrad searched each others faces, both thinking. *"I can't believe she just said that."*

"A bit surprised, are we ?" spouted Joyce. "I knew you would figure it out sooner or later. As it turned out it was sooner. And that was probably due to having the good sense to get a woman to help you.

Mark, Hank and Susan were all staring at Joyce in disbelief. First of all for speaking the way she did and secondly for obviously admitting to the murder or murders. Joyce continued cheerfully.

"Yes, I am admitting to killing that bitch Florence."

"What about Norman Holt and Cynthia Hopkins." asked Dwyer after recovering from Joyce's admission and finally finding his voice.

"Oh, yeah, them too. They would eventually have gotten in my way." she said off handedly.

"Why ? Ms. Lambertson, if you don't mind me asking. Why such brutal murders." inquired Susan.

Joyce now looking to the two men again replied.

"See what I mean, it takes a woman to get right to the point."

In the meantime Susan had positioned herself in front of the door while Hank and Mark were obliquely to either side of Joyce yet a fair distance away.

"I guess that's a reasonable question. The police always want a motive don't they. Okay, let's start with the Goodwyn dragon lady."

"I take it you didn't like the woman." Hank was stating the obvious.

For the first time since she opened the door Joyce was not smiling when she answered.

"That witch killed my mother and sister. I just gave her what she had coming to her."

Joyce's attitude was a bit of a surprise to Hank and Mark. More like a shock to Susan who was not accustomed to dealing direct with people . "When   did   this   occur." Mark questioned professionally.

Joyce eyed Dwyer and tilting her head and with a slight sneer she stated clearly;

"When I was eight years old. Now I suppose you're going to ask why did I carry this hate so long. I'll tell you why." her voice rising a little. "My mother and sister were the only family I had. There were no other relatives to take me in so I became a ward of the state and they put me in a home. I don't care about all the good things they tell the public but that place was a living hell. The longer I was there the more I wanted to get even with that Florence Goodwyn."

Susan was having a hard time trying to digest her story. *"I don't know how Mark and Hank do this on a daily basis. I love what I do and now I know I'll keep doing it."* she mentally told herself.

"But that was so long ago, didn't you learn about forgiveness." Susan asked calmly.

Joyce snapped her head around to Mark.

"I learned survival in the home. That's all I learned. That's all life is, survival. And I survived to get even."

"And what about the consequences you now face because of your rash actions."

Smiling again she replied;

"Well, that's life, isn't it. I told you it's all about survival. I'm satisfied that I did what I had to."

Hank, out of pure curiosity asked;

" If you were only eight at the time how did you ever find her in the big city. I keep telling you, survival. That's the key to everything. I guess I was playing detective like you. If you keep asking questions you eventually get answers. Well, I finally got my answers. To my advantage she didn't recognize me when I applied for the job at the library.

Hank now asked, " Why did you kill her in such a brutal way."

"That's easy to answer, I wanted her to suffer just as I had for all those years in the home without a family." She emphasized the last word.

There was a short pause which everyone used to digest what they just heard.

"Ms. Lambertson." Susan asked calmly. She was interrupted right away.

"Joyce, if you don't mind."

"As you wish." Susan continued. Joyce, we found traces of drugs in the blood. Was that necessary and where did you acquire them.

"Where is of no consequence, I told you, survival. The why of it, I wasn't sure how strong Florence was or was not, so I thought I may need some help."

"And is that why you recruited Norman ?" Mark inquired.

"Yes, nice touch, don't you think. He was so easy to control and manipulate. You know, I think he was still a virgin. That is until I got hold of him." Joyce was almost laughing. I believe I could have had him kill the President if I wanted. He was such a nerd."

"Well, if you could control him so easily, why kill him."

"I had my doubts about how long he would keep quiet, So I decided it would be easier to do away with loose ends. The little twerp was easier to handle than the witch."

"This is really unbelievable." thought Susan.

Another short pause while Joyce made herself comfortable on the sofa..

"Oh, forgive me, I'm forgetting my manners. Would anyone care for a drink ? Oh no, you're working. How about coffee or tea. I usually enjoy an afternoon tea.

The team could not get over the fact of how blasé Joyce was treating this whole thing. The offer of refreshments was politely turned down and Mark pursued another question.

"Harold Twining, what made you try to implicate him."

Joyce smiled again thinking how much fun that was. "It just seemed like the thing to do at the time. He was so stiff and proper all the time. I overheard him on the phone talking to some guy about going tp Philly in his place because something else came up that was more important."

Dwyer and Conrad looked at each other trying not to smile knowing what they knew. Joyce pushed on.

"Once I heard that I knew it would fit in with my plans rather well. It almost worked." She gave a slight laugh.

Another short pause which seemed like forever to Blake, Conrad and Dwyer, then Joyce resumed her open confession.

"Then, of course there was Cynthia. Probably the only real friend I ever had."

Gazing now at the three police persons she admitted, "We grew up together in the home. She was so innocent and helpless. All the other kids picked on her no end. That is , until I started defending her. As I mentioned, SURVIVAL. That's the key."

"So that's why Cynthia looked so happy when she saw Joyce at the airport. Joyce was a true friend to her." this memory ran through Mark's mind.

"Well we both survived, thanks to me. I honestly did not enjoy killing her but- - - - ."

"Then why did you ?' Asked Sgt. Dwyer.

Turning towards Mark she answered slowly.

"Well, I know she took a liking to you and that you had even asked her to dinner."

Hearing this disappointed Susan. She felt a sudden hurt and much disappointment. She hoped she didn't let it show.

"I knew how weak she was and did not want to take the chance of her slipping up with you. It really did bother me to kill her. I guess I loved her more than I thought."

Joyce's face reflected her inner emotions for a short second . She right away snapped herself out of it. Now back to her smile and not give a damn attitude.

"Well, that about covers it." she said standing. "Any other questions ?" looking at all three Sgts. "Oh, there is one other piece of information you should know about. I wasn't sure whether or not you would be recording my confession so I set it up myself. In that stereo cabinet you will find that this whole fun time was being recorded. The tape is yours with my compliments."

Hank was closest and turned around to view the cabinet. Mark also moved closer stretching to get a look.

"I guess there is nothing left but to say goodbye to this place." Joyce laughed.

With that she ran. It was amazing the speed she attained in such a short amount of space. She bounded on to the sofa catapulting herself through the large picture window out into the night. Just before she hit the couch Susan yelled.

"Mark !"

It was already too late. The noise of the smashing glass drew his and Hank's immediate attention. After that it was just the sound of silence. Within moments that seemed like hours, a commotion was heard below.

The sound of the smashing glass drew the young officer barging through th door almost sending Susan sprawling. Instantly reacting Hank yelled, "Officer with me." as he headed toward the elevator. Susan was close on his heels. Mark was already on the phone to emergency services. He also then headed down.

~ ~ ~ ~ ~ ~

Later that night in the forensics lab, Mark, Hank and Susan were making the best of coffee and stale donuts trying to rationalize the evening they just participated in.

Captain Braddick joined them briefly with words of

encouragement then politely ordered them all to go home to bed. There were no arguments. Hank departed without hesitation. As Susan and Mark were leaving she handed Mark a paper with her address and phone number.

"I'm not on call for the next two days."

She gazed deeply into his eyes, smiled lightly, turned and walked away. Mark stood there following with his eyes asking himself. *"Have I been missing something?."*

Day eight

Even though he was given a few days off, Mark was in his office early on Monday. The uneasiness of yesterdays events were nagging at the back of his mind. He actually felt sorry for Joyce. It was obviously the system that let her down. That was a totally unnecessary burden for a youngster to carry, and to carry for so long.

For what ever reason he felt compelled to research the death of her mother and sister. He remembered she mentioned a town in Ohio where she grew up. Closing the office door for privacy he reached for the phone. Without too much trouble he made contact with the local town police. He inquired about the death's of Joyce's mother and sister. As luck would have it small town records were less difficult to track than in a big city. The logistics of storage was far less complicated.

By noon he had an answer.

It had been an auto accident. Florence Goodwyn was driving the car that broadsided the Lambertson's vehicle. <u>But</u>, it was not her fault. The Lambertson vehicle driven by Joyce's mother while under the influence, ran a red light. It was unavoidable. There were seven witnesses. Joyce was in the back seat on the far side and was unharmed.

"Poor kid." thought Mark. *"Carrying all that hate and obviously not the correct story for all those years."*

Joyce was right in one thing. The system let her down.

Sgt. Dwyer filed this report along with the rest of the case file. He knew it really wasn't part of the case, but in an odd sort of way it was.

He sat back, noticed the wall clock said one o' five. He rested a bit his mind still working. He reached for the paper Susan gave him and dialed her number.

The End

www.ingramcontent.com/pod-product-compliance
Lightning Source LLC
Chambersburg PA
CBHW022016120726
47902CB00012B/474